MADELINE

D0488295

Also by Ludwig Bemelmans

HERE is a list for those who may wish to identify the Paris scenes Ludwig Bemelmans has pictured in this book.

On the cover and in one of the illustrations
THE EIFFEL TOWER

In the picture of the lady feeding the horse
THE OPERA

A gendarme chases a jewel thief across
THE PLACE VENDOME

A wounded soldier at
THE HOTEL DES INVALIDES

A rainy day in front of
NOTRE DAME

A sunny day looking across
THE GARDENS AT THE LUXEMBOURG

Behind the little girls skating is
THE CHURCH OF THE SACRE COEUR

A man is feeding birds in
THE TUILERIES GARDENS FACING THE LOUVRE

MADELINE

story & pictures by
Ludwig Bemelmans

Hippo

Scholastic Children's Books,
7-9 Pratt Street, London NW1 0AE, UK
a division of Scholastic Ltd
London ~ New York ~ Toronto ~ Sydney ~ Auckland

First published in the UK by André Deutsch Limited, 1952
This edition published in the UK by Scholastic Ltd, 1996

Copyright © Ludwig Bemelmans, 1952

Copyright renewed © Madeleine Bemelmans and
Barbara Bemelmans Marciano, 1989

All rights reserved

ISBN 0 590 13337 3

10 9 8 7 6 5 4 3 2 1

This book is sold subject to the condition that it shall not, by way of trade or
otherwise be lent, resold, hired out, or otherwise circulated without the
publisher's prior consent in any form of binding or cover other than that
in which it is published and without a similar condition, including this
condition, being imposed upon the subsequent purchaser.

In an old house in Paris

that was covered with vines

lived twelve little girls in two straight lines.

In two straight lines they broke their bread

and brushed their teeth

and went to bed.

They smiled at the good

and frowned at the bad

and sometimes they were very sad.

They left the house

at half past nine

in two straight lines

in rain

or shine—

the smallest one was Madeline.

She was not afraid of mice—

she loved winter, snow, and ice.

To the tiger in the zoo
Madeline just said, "Pooh-pooh,"

and nobody knew so well
how to frighten Miss Clavel.

In the middle of the night
Miss Clavel turned on the light
and said, "Something is not right!"

Little Madeline sat in bed,

cried and cried; her eyes were red.

And soon after Dr. Cohn

came, he rushed out to the phone

and he dialed: DANton-ten-six—

"Nurse," he said, "it's an appendix!"

Everybody had to cry—
not a single eye was dry.

Madeline was in his arm
in a blanket safe and warm.

In a car with a red light

they drove out into the night.

Madeline woke up two hours
later, in a room with flowers.

Madeline soon ate and drank.

On her bed there was a crank,

and a crack on the ceiling had the habit
of sometimes looking like a rabbit.

Outside were birds, trees, and sky—
and so ten days passed quickly by.

One nice morning Miss Clavel said—

"Isn't this a fine—

day to visit

Madeline.”

VISITORS FROM TWO TO FOUR
read a sign outside her door.

Tiptoeing with solemn face,

with some flowers and a vase,

in they walked and then said, "Ahhh,"
when they saw the toys and candy
and the dollhouse from Papa.

But the biggest surprise by far—

on her stomach

was a scar!

"Good-bye," they said, "we'll come again,"

and the little girls left in the rain.

They went home and broke their bread

brushed their teeth

and went to bed.

In the middle of one night
Miss Clavel turned on her light
and said, "Something is not right!"

And afraid of a disaster

Miss Clavel ran fast

and faster,

and she said, "Please children do—
tell me what is troubling you?"

And all the little girls cried, "Boohoo,
we want to have our appendix out, too!"

"Good night, little girls!
Thank the lord you are well!
And now go to sleep!"
said Miss Clavel.

And she turned out the light—
and closed the door—
and that's all there is—
there isn't any more.